The Shakespeare

A MIDSUMMER NIGHT'S DREAM

RETOLD BY CLARE BEVAN

Illustrated by Ross Collins

OXFORD
UNIVERSITY PRESS

 *Character list:*

THE ATHENIANS

Duke Theseus
(ruler of Athens)

Hippolyta
(his bride to be)

Hermia

Egeus
(Hermia's father)

Helena
(Hermia's best friend)

Lysander

Demetrius

THE WORKMEN

Peter Quince
(carpenter)

Francis Flute
(bellows mender)

Tom Snout
(tinker)

Robin Starveling
(tailor)

Snug
(joiner)

Nick Bottom
(weaver)

THE FAIRIES

Oberon
(fairy king)

Puck
(sprite)

Titania
(fairy queen)

Titania's fairies

Centuries ago, in the city of Athens, there lived a wise duke named Theseus. He was planning an amazing wedding party for his warrior bride, Hippolyta. At the feast there would be music and laughter and dancing!

Suddenly, into the palace burst a group of young people, led by a grumpy nobleman. His name was Egeus, and he was a father with a stony heart.

"You must punish my disobedient daughter," he demanded, pointing at a small, dark-haired girl called Hermia. "I have found her a fine husband, young Demetrius here. But she says she loves Lysander, and will marry no one else."

Egeus was sure he would win the argument. You see, in those days there was a strict and harsh law, which said that a girl must marry the man her parents had chosen for her. If she refused, the punishment might be death!

Theseus understood the power of love and he pitied Hermia, but he could only offer her three terrible choices.

"Obey your father and live. Obey your heart and die. Or become a nun and forget about weddings forever," he said with a sigh.

Poor Hermia and Lysander were given just enough time to say goodbye to one another. But their eyes shone as they whispered together, because Lysander had already worked out a clever plan.

"Meet me in the woods tomorrow night," he said, under his breath. "And we'll run away to my old aunty's house. The laws of Athens can't reach us there, so we'll be able to marry each other after all."

Perhaps that would have been the end of the story, if they hadn't bumped into Helena. She was a tall, slender girl whose beauty was clouded by jealousy. And no wonder! Demetrius had loved her until he met Hermia.

"Don't be sad," Hermia told her friend kindly. "You can have Demetrius all to yourself as soon as I've escaped with Lysander." And in moments the secret was out.

As soon as Helena was alone, she smiled. "I'll tell Demetrius everything," she promised herself. "And maybe he'll love me again."

*I*n a poorer part of the city, Quince, the carpenter, was making plans, too. He and his friends were preparing a play for the duke's wedding day. The workmen were all bursting with excitement, but first Quince needed to give out the parts.

This was going to be tricky, because Bottom, the weaver, wanted to play them all! The hero, Pyramus, the tragic girlfriend, Thisbe – even the savage lion.

"I can shout. I can whisper. I can roar!" he cried. And to prove it, he started to recite pages of poetry.

"The raging rocks,
With shivering shocks..."

Even when Quince persuaded him to play Pyramus, Bottom still wanted to talk about himself.

"What sort of beard shall I wear? Orange? Purple? Bright yellow?" he wondered.

It was too late for a rehearsal now. The tired workmen planned to meet in the woods the next night. Quince and Flute. Snout and Starveling. Quiet Snug and noisy Bottom.

$\mathcal{A}$ whole day flew by like a summer's breeze. The woods glimmered under the stars, and among the trees fairies' wings flickered in the moonlight. The night was their special time, and this was their special place. The fairy king and queen were due to arrive at any minute, and the silver leaves would rustle with spells.

But someone was troubled. It was Puck,
the naughtiest, cheekiest sprite of them all.

"My master, King Oberon, has quarrelled
with Queen Titania," he warned one of the fairies
as he whirled across the grass. "And all because
of a tiny, orphaned boy. Titania owns the boy;
Oberon wants him as a henchman. They must
not meet, or there will be bad magic in the air
tonight..."

But before Puck could stop them, the king
and queen swept into the clearing. When they
saw each other, hatred flashed in their fiery eyes.

"Ill met by moonlight, proud Titania,"
snarled Oberon. And the two spirits spat insults
at each other until the queen flounced away with
her fairy followers.

Hungry for revenge, the fairy king summoned
Puck to his side. "In a far land there grows an
enchanted flower," said Oberon. "One drop of its
juice on the Queen's sleeping eyes will make her
fall in love with the first living creature that she
sees. Find that flower and bring it to me!"

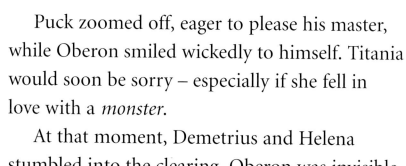

Puck zoomed off, eager to please his master, while Oberon smiled wickedly to himself. Titania would soon be sorry – especially if she fell in love with a *monster*.

At that moment, Demetrius and Helena stumbled into the clearing. Oberon was invisible to them, but he listened to their every word.

"I can't help being attracted to you," wailed Helena, as Demetrius pushed her roughly aside. "Please let me follow you like a pet spaniel."

"Go home," he snapped in disgust. "I'm looking for Hermia. And I intend to find her." With that he hurried away, while Helena scurried after him.

The fairy king was struck by Helena's sadness. I'll make her happy with my magic flower, he thought. So when Puck whizzed back from his whirlwind journey, Oberon sent him after the Athenian man and the lonely lady. With him Puck carried a purple petal to charm the heartless lover's eyes.

As for Oberon, he flew to a mossy bank where the wild thyme trembled. And there he found Titania, sound asleep among the violets and roses. He raised his flower and squeezed it softly over her eyelids, to set the potion free.

Drip, drop! The deed was done, and Oberon crooned a wicked wish into her rippling hair. "Wake when some *vile* thing is near!"

Close by, Lysander and Hermia staggered happily through the twisted branches.

"We're safe from your father now," yawned Lysander. "Let's rest here."

"Not too close together," Hermia warned him. "We aren't married yet." So they each curled up on a cushion of leaves and fell into a deep and dreamy sleep.

If only they had known that Puck was passing by, and about to make a dreadful mistake. But it was too late. He had seen them.

"This must be the Athenian I was sent to find," he said. And he splashed a little of the flower's juice on to the young man's lashes.

Now, this wouldn't have mattered if Lysander had woken to see Hermia. But he didn't. Instead it was Helena who came crashing through the bushes, still trying to catch her dear Demetrius.

"Lysander!" she yelped in surprise.

He opened his eyes. Wide. And sighed. And fell instantly in love with Helena!

"Sweet Helena," he gasped, "I love you. And *only* you."

Helena glared angrily at him. "Don't tease me," she shouted. "Everyone knows that you belong to Hermia."

"Not any more," protested Lysander. And he trailed after her as she stamped into the green darkness.

Seconds later, Hermia sat up with a scream. "Help me, Lysander! I've had a terrible nightmare, and—"

But where was Lysander? Had he been mauled by wild beasts? Or murdered by cruel Demetrius? In panic she called her sweetheart's name, and ran, and ran through the forest.

Disaster! Demetrius was chasing Hermia, who was chasing Lysander, who was chasing Helena, who was chasing Demetrius, who was...

Everything was quiet and calm where Queen Titania lay on her bed of blossoms. But nothing lasts for long and soon the woodland echoed to the sound of clumping boots. Quince's band of rowdy workmen were ready to start their rehearsal.

"Wait a minute," gulped Bottom. "What if the delicate ladies are frightened when Pyramus brandishes his sword? We'd better write a speech to explain it's not real."

Suddenly the others were worried too. What about the roaring lion? And how were they supposed to make Starveling look like moonshine? Or turn Snout into a solid wall?

They would have worried even more if they had known that Puck was watching them. Silent as a shadow he waited for his chance, and as soon as Bottom strode by Puck cast a spell over him.

In an instant, Bottom was wearing a donkey's head – and he had no idea!

When they saw him, Bottom's friends ran away in terror.

"What's up, lads?" he called, but he was all alone. So he clopped up and down, braying a loud song to hide his fears.

"The finch, the sparrow and the lark..." he sang, out of tune.

The awful noise he made woke Titania, who stretched like a cat, yawned elegantly, and fell in love with Bottom at first sight.

They made a very odd couple – the fairy queen and the hairy donkey.

Bottom could hardly believe his luck, especially when he was given his own troop of fairy servants, Cobweb, Peas-Blossom, Moth and Mustardseed. "Maybe the world has turned upside down," he sighed to himself. "But I don't mind."

$\mathcal{P}$uck, of course, was thrilled with himself. He couldn't wait to tell his master the news. "The queen loves a fool," he crowed, "and the man from Athens has stars in his eyes."

Oberon listened with pleasure, until he heard the sound of angry voices.

Hermia had spotted Demetrius, the man she loathed. "Where is my Lysander?" she yelled. "Have you killed him?"

"N-N-No," stammered Demetrius. "You're mistaken." But she had already gone, and he sank down – too sleepy to follow her.

Puck was puzzled. "Right girl, wrong man," he muttered.

But Oberon saw through the muddle at once. "Wrong girl, right man. This is all your fault, Puck. You must have used my flower on a different Athenian." So the sprite was sent to find Helena while the king touched the young man's eyelids with his wonderful flower.

Puck sped away like an arrow from a bow, and swiftly returned with Helena. Unfortunately, she came with Lysander in tow!

Demetrius woke at once, and Oberon's enchantment worked like a dream. "Helena," he cried. "You are a princess! A goddess!"

But Helena was not impressed. "Why do you insult me?" she said bitterly. "Everyone knows that you hate me."

"Not any more," protested Demetrius. "I love you. Truly I do."

And that was when Hermia arrived. With a sigh of relief, she rushed to Lysander's side, expecting a hug, a kiss, a smile...

"Go away," he said coldly. Puck's magic potion still stung his eyes. "Can't you see? I love *Helena*, not you."

Hermia was hurt. Confused. Astonished. She had risked her life for Lysander and now he had turned against her. To make matters worse, Demetrius seemed to dislike her, too. "This must be Helena's fault," she decided.

Helena was equally upset. "They're all lying to me. Laughing behind my back. Pretending to love me. This nasty game must be Hermia's idea."

In no time tall Helena and little Hermia were shrieking names at each other.

"Puppet!"

"Painted maypole!"

Meanwhile, the two men drew their swords to fight for Helena's sake. And Puck, perched above them, hugged himself with delight.

Oberon, however, had seen quite enough
chaos for one night. "Cast a spell of confusion,"
he ordered Puck. "Torment and tire them all."

"Up and down, up and down, I will lead
them up and down." Puck sang merrily, as a
phantom fog billowed around the fighting men.

Suddenly Demetrius and Lysander were hearing strange voices. Running from shadows. Stabbing at thorn bushes. They gave themselves a thousand frights, until finally they collapsed on the moss like exhausted children.

The ladies had also been led astray. Helena stumbled into the same glade, too weary with weeping to notice the young men. And last came heart-broken Hermia, stained and scratched, still murmuring her lost love's name.

When all four were safely asleep, Puck charmed Lysander's eyes one last time.

At daybreak he would wake to see Hermia's face, and she would be loved again.

The queen and donkey-headed Bottom were still snuggled together on their flowery bank, but King Oberon was about to release them from their enchantment, too. Titania had given him the little boy he wanted, so now he touched her eyelids with a kindly spell. As soon as she opened her eyes and saw who she had been cuddling, Titania shrieked and clung to Oberon. This was just what he'd planned.

Hand in hand they disappeared into the
dawn, while Puck was left to change Bottom
back into his breezy old self.

The day dawned brightly. The sound of music and barking dogs rang through the forest. It was the duke's wedding day, and the woods were full of huntsmen. Theseus and Hippolyta were enjoying the chase until Egeus arrived, grumpier than ever. He had just spotted his daughter, muddy and bedraggled, sleeping on the ground beside Lysander.

But why were Helena and Demetrius there as well? The sleepers began to wake up. They rubbed their eyes and stared at each other. Their night fears had faded and all was well.

Lysander loved Hermia more than before and told her father so. But then, to everyone's amazement, up jumped Demetrius crying, "As for me, I truly love Helena. Today and *forever*." And with these words, he set Hermia free.

Egeus, as usual, was demanding death penalties, but Theseus came up with a much happier plan.

"Away you run," he told the four lovers with a smile. "Today there shall be *three* weddings instead of just one!"

While they were pulling on their best clothes and combing the tangles from their hair, Bottom was hurrying home, his big head swarming with magical memories.

The other workmen were feeling very low. No
Bottom meant no show. No fame. And no fee
either. But just as they were about to give up
hope, his cheery face appeared at the door.

"Come on, lads," he boomed. "Grab your
gear. Don't delay. I'm told the duke is ready
for a play."

*A*t the palace, the party was in full swing. Hermia was with Lysander. Helena was beside Demetrius. And Theseus was trying to choose the perfect entertainment to please Hippolyta.

The list was rather dreary. Only one item tickled his imagination: *The Tragical Comedy of Pyramus and Thisbe* – Bottom's play. It sounded peculiar, but the duke guessed the play had been put together with good intentions, so he made his decision: Bottom and Company!

Quince began in such a flutter, he made a total mess of his opening speech. Then Snout staggered on stage in his clumsy wall costume, Bottom waved his wooden blade, and Flute did his best to look like a dainty maiden, even though he was sprouting a beard.

The guests were having a glorious time. They laughed at Moonshine with his lantern and dog. They smiled at Lion's tiny, timid roars. They loved the part where Thisbe was chased around the floor. And they cheered while Pyramus killed himself very, *very*, slowly.

At last the pantomime ended, the band played and the workmen performed a jolly dance. It had all been a great success.

*M*idnight struck, and darkness swooped down.

The crowds vanished. The brides and their new husbands stole away to the sound of fairy music, while Oberon and Titania wove spells of joy to keep them happy ever after. And what about Puck, that mischief-maker? He sat alone under the starry sky.

Because the dream was over. The story told.